John Riddel

TARO AND THE TŌFU

A PAIR OF RED CLOGS *By the same author*

Taro

MASAKO MATSUNO

and the Tōfu

Illustrated by KAZUE MIZUMURA

THE WORLD PUBLISHING COMPANY

CLEVELAND AND NEW YORK

WEEKLY READER BOOK CLUB EDITION

PUBLISHED BY The World Publishing Company
2231 West 110th Street, Cleveland 2, Ohio

PUBLISHED SIMULTANEOUSLY IN CANADA BY
NELSON, FOSTER & SCOTT LTD.

Library of Congress Catalog Card Number: 62–9058

FIRST EDITION

COHW

1 2 3 4 65 64 63 6

For my first son

It was windy.

The wind was cold.

The cold, windy day was growing into a cold, windy night. From the window where he was watching for the *tōfu* seller, Taro could see the evening star already twinkling in the eastern sky.

Tōfu is Japanese for what is called "bean curd" in English. It is white, and shaped like a small cake. It is soft and cool to the touch. And it is very nourishing, so it is one of the most important foods of the Japanese people.

Usually, Taro's mother bought *tōfu* from an old peddler who came along the street every evening. "Pooo... Pooo . . . Poooooo . . ." his trumpet sounded, calling his wares.

Other *tōfu* sellers came along the street, too.

> "P P PPPP Poooooo . . ." But that wasn't the old man's trumpet.
> "Poooooooo . . . P P P Poo . . ." wasn't his call either.
> "Pooo . . . Pooo . . . Poooooo . . ."

"Here he comes," Taro's mother would say. "He is poor, but his bean curd is the best of all." And she always bought *tōfu* from the old man.

But on this cold, windy evening the old man did not come.

"P P PPPP Poooooo . . ." sounded.
"Poooooooo . . . P P P Poo . . ." sounded, too.
But not "Pooo . . . Pooo . . . Poooooo . . ."

In the snug, warm kitchen Taro and his mother waited and waited, listening to each seller's trumpet until at last it was time to cook supper.

"I wonder what has happened to him," said Taro's mother. "This is the first time he hasn't come without letting us know."

"Shall I run to his shop?" asked Taro.

His mother hesitated. "It's getting dark . . . and cold, too."

"That's all right," said Taro. "It's not so late yet, is it? I'll get the *tōfu* for you, Mother."

From beyond the village shrine woods, the cold wind blew. Taro, clutching a small pan for *tōfu* in one hand and a silver coin in the other, began running as soon as he left the house.

The shopping street was crowded with people buying good food for supper. The shops were light and gay.

"Come in and buy! Come in and buy! My fish are fresh!" a loud voice called from a fish store.

"Stop, boy! Can't you smell my roasted yams?" a young sweet-potato seller shouted at Taro.

But Taro didn't stop. This wasn't the place he was

looking for. The old man's shop was much farther along
the street, away from the main shopping place. That was
why he went to the houses every evening to sell his *tōfu*.

Taro bumped and jostled his way through the crowd.
Beyond the lights and noise of the shops it was cold and
dark and lonely. Only one dim light showed at the very
end of the street. It was the light of the old man's shop.

The old man was surprised to see Taro. "Are you alone?" he asked. "Did you come here all by yourself?"

"Yes, *ojiisan* (old man), my mother needs two cakes of *tōfu*. She waited a long time for you to come, but you didn't come. What happened?"

The old man took the *tōfu* pan Taro was holding out to him. "I'm sorry," he said. "My grandson doesn't feel well today, so I couldn't leave him alone. But I'll come to your house tomorrow evening, as usual," the old man added, handing Taro the filled *tōfu* pan, "so you won't have to come down in the cold."

"How much?" asked Taro.

"Thirty yen."

Taro handed the coin to the old man, who slowly counted out the change under the dim light of the shop.

"Thank you, Taro," he said. "You'd better hurry home. Your mother must be waiting for you."

"Yes. Good-by!"

"Don't run, Taro!" the old man shouted after him. "My *tōfu* is soft and delicate. Carry it carefully so it doesn't break!"

Pitcha . . . Pitcha . . . Pitcha . . . Top . . . Top . . . Top . . . The water which keeps bean-curd cakes soft and moist sloshed in the pan Taro held carefully against his chest. Sometimes he lifted the *tōfu* pan high above his head so it wouldn't be bumped by the crowd and the delicate bean curd broken. But he walked fast, too. Whenever he did an errand for his mother he was allowed to keep 10 yen for himself, and he was in a hurry to get to the little candy store on the main shopping street.

The candy store was run by an old lady with big glasses who always sat in a far corner of the shop reading a newspaper. She rarely spoke more than a few words to her customers. "Thank you, good boy," or "Thank you, good girl," she would say, never looking up from her paper. It was one of the seven wonders to Taro how she knew a boy was a boy—or a girl, a girl—without ever looking at them.

And the old lady never seemed to mind if the children took a long time to decide what to buy with their pocket money. It made Taro feel that all the candies in the store belonged to him until at last the moment came to decide exactly what to buy.

Sugar beans, chocolate candies,
salted beans, chewing gum . . .

Taro had to decide quickly today so he could hurry home with the *tōfu*.

Two packages of chocolate, he said to himself, putting his hand in his pocket for the change the old man had given him. Taro picked one of the coins to give to the old lady.

But, wait, it was a 50-yen coin!

Where did I get this?

Taro looked at the coin in surprise. I thought the old man gave me seven 10-yen coins, for the *tōfu* was 30 yen, and I gave him a 100-yen coin. One, two, three, four, five, six . . . Here are six 10-yen coins and a 50-yen . . . Then the old man made a mistake. I must return the extra 40 yen to him right away. He will worry if he finds he has lost money.

But outside it was already dark and the wind was harsh.

"It's getting late, and very cold . . ." a strange little voice whispered inside Taro's head. "Why not tomorrow? Even if the old man worries, the mistake is his own fault. It's very cold, and Mother must be waiting," the secret voice continued.

Taro looked at the money in his hand, and then at the cold outdoors. "It's just the same whether you give the money back tonight or tomorrow," whispered the voice again. "Besides, who knows that you've got the extra money? No one need know. Imagine, with forty extra yen to spend, you could buy sugar beans and salted beans and chocolate and chewing gum and even more. . . . Right?"

Oh, no—it was almost a shout inside him—no, no, it's not right. This is not my money. It belongs to the old man, even if it was his fault that he gave me the wrong change. I don't want the candies and chewing gum! Taro was talking to himself very fast now, as if he was in a hurry to rid himself of the strange, secret voice inside his head. I will return the money right now.

"*Obasan!* (Miss!)" Taro called to the lady of the candy store. But his voice sounded so dry and cracked that only a little husky whisper came out.

"*Obasan!*" he called once more. "I'll take two packages of chocolate candy today."

"Thank you, good boy," answered the lady, without looking up.

Taro smiled. "And may I leave my *tōfu* pan here for just a little while?" he asked.

"Of course you may, good boy," answered the old lady, still looking at her newspaper.

Taro put his *tōfu* pan carefully on the counter with a 10-yen coin for the candies and ran out of the store. He ran down the gay shopping street, zigzagging through the crowds of people. He was still running when he reached the little shop where the old man was bending over a big tub of *tōfu*.

"Back so soon?" said the man, seeing Taro. "Does your mother need more *tōfu*?"

"No. I came to give this money back to you," said Taro, panting.

"What money?"

"You gave me the wrong change. Forty extra yen."

"Really? I didn't notice it. Are you sure the money isn't yours?"

"Yes, I'm sure. You gave me a fifty-yen coin instead of a ten-yen coin. I'll put the money here. All right? I must hurry; Mother is waiting for me."

"Thank you very much, Taro," said the old man with gladness in his face.

Taro was happy, but he was embarrassed too, for he remembered the strange little voice.

"Not at all," he said quickly. Before he knew it, he found himself taking one of the packages of chocolate candy from his pocket. "For your grandson, *ojiisan*," he said.

"Thank you. . . . Thank you. . . ."

The old lady in the candy store was still reading her newspaper when Taro stopped to pick up the *tōfu* pan.

"Thank you for keeping it for me," said Taro.

"Not at all, good boy," said the lady, and much to Taro's surprise she looked straight at him.

Taro had never seen her look at anything except her newspaper. What was more, she was smiling at him behind her big glasses, almost as if she knew what had happened. But, no, it couldn't be possible!

"You'd better hurry, good boy. It's very late," said the lady.

Taro nodded and went out of the store with his *tōfu* pan.

Most of the shops on the shopping street were closed now, and only a few people still lingered there. The wind was very cold.

Anyway, thought Taro, it doesn't matter if the lady knows what the voice said. Because I gave back the money.

He was so happy that he wanted to run all the way home, but he remembered to walk carefully with the old man's delicate *tōfu*. Pitcha . . . Pitcha . . . Top . . . Top . . . The water in the pan sloshed softly and rhythmically, as if it was trying to match Taro's light spirit.

In the warm, cozy kitchen Taro told his parents what had happened to make him so late. He told them about finding the extra 40 yen, and he told them about returning to the old man's shop. He told them everything . . . except he didn't tell them about the strange, secret voice in his head. Nor did he tell them about giving the candy to the old man's sick grandson. Why? I don't know. Taro just felt like keeping those things to himself, I think.

"May I have a chocolate candy now?" he asked.

"Yes, but just one. Supper is almost ready," said his mother, stirring the *tōfu* into the delicious-smelling soup.

It was still windy outside. And the wind was cold.
Yes, I have told you it was a cold, windy night, haven't I?
But Taro felt warm. And the chocolate candy tasted
good, you know.